The Willow Umbrella

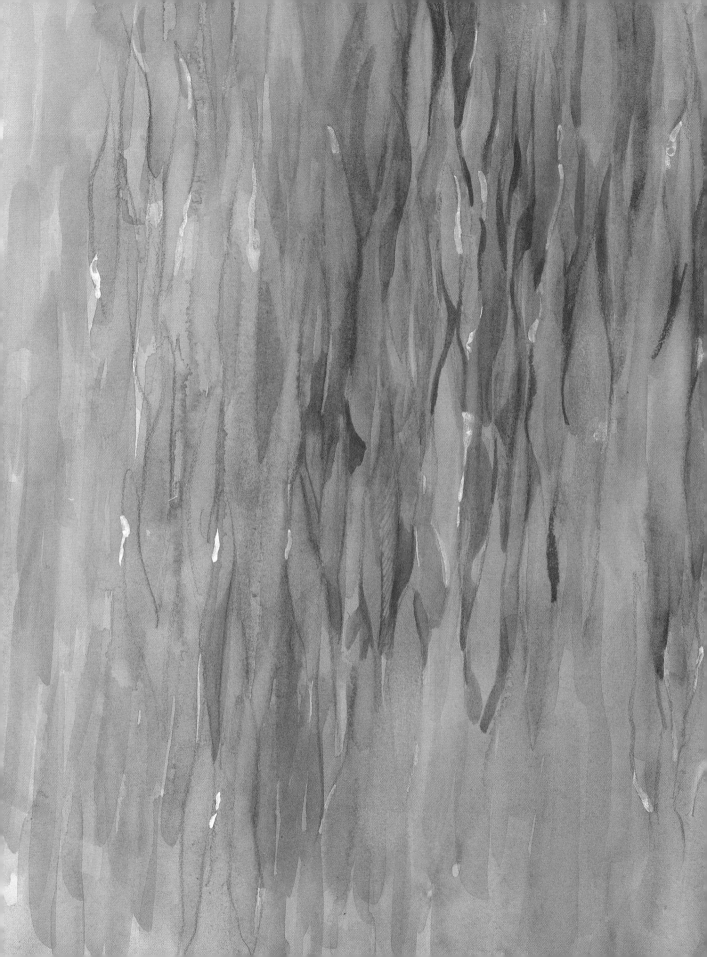

The Willow Umbrella

by Christine Widman

illustrated by Catherine Stock

MACMILLAN PUBLISHING COMPANY   New York

Maxwell Macmillan Canada   Toronto

Maxwell Macmillan International   New York   Oxford   Singapore   Sydney

Text copyright © 1993 by Christine Widman
Illustrations copyright © 1993 by Catherine Stock
All rights reserved. No part of this book may be reproduced or transmitted in any form or by any
means, electronic or mechanical, including photocopying, recording, or by any information storage and
retrieval system, without permission in writing from the Publisher.
Macmillan Publishing Company is part of the Maxwell Communication Group of Companies.
Macmillan Publishing Company, 866 Third Avenue, New York, NY 10022.
Maxwell Macmillan Canada, Inc., 1200 Eglinton Avenue East, Suite 200, Don Mills, Ontario M3C 3N1.
First edition
Printed in the United States of America
1   3   5   7   9   10   8   6   4   2
The text of this book is set in 16 pt. Kennerly.
The illustrations are rendered in watercolor.

Library of Congress Cataloging-in-Publication Data
Widman, Christine Barker. The willow umbrella / by Christine Widman ; illustrated by Catherine
Stock. — 1st ed.   p.   cm.   Summary: Two little girls discover how much fun it can be to play
in the rain.   ISBN 0-02-792760-1   [1. Rain and rainfall—Fiction.]   I. Stock, Catherine,
ill.   II. Title.   PZ7.W6346Wi   1993   [E]—dc20   91-10989

To my mother, with love

and

to my cousin, Kathy,

with thanks for my hollyhock summers

—C. W.

For Zoë and Helena

—C. S.

It's raining.
Ashley watches the raindrops slip down
the branches of the willow tree.
She wanted to play dolls with Rebecca
under the willow today.
Rain, rain go away.

It's pouring.
Ashley is tired of painting watercolor pictures.
The colors blur together and remind her that
it's raining.
She rocks back and forth in the kitchen rocker.
The creaking of the rocker says,
Raindrops, raindrops.
Rain, go away.
Come again another day.

Ashley sees Rebecca coming down the street.
She's holding a yellow umbrella.
It looks like the sun Ashley painted in her picture.
She wishes Rebecca were bringing the sun
so they could play dolls under the willow tree.
Rain, rain go away. Ashley wants to play.

She waves to Rebecca.
"Hurry up…come in. We have to play inside today."

"No, we don't. Come out! Let's walk in the rain."

Ashley squeezes close to Rebecca under
the yellow umbrella.
The air is wet and warm.
The sidewalk is shiny like a gray satin sash.

Rebecca stops.
"What are you doing?" asks Ashley.
"Shh," says Rebecca.
"Do you hear the rain sounds?"

Drip…drip. Rain falls from the leaves.
Plish—splash. It runs down the rainspout.
Tat tat tat tat. The rain taps on the umbrella.

"It sounds like tiny horses galloping,"
says Rebecca.
"Palominos prancing on the yellow umbrella."
"No," says Ashley. "Dapple-grays, like the rain."

The girls start to walk again.
A gust of wind blows leaves
in a whirl around them.

Ashley picks up a leaf and drops it into a river
the rain has made in the street.
The leaf rides the rainwater like
a thin green canoe.

"Do you want to go in and play dolls now?"
asks Rebecca.
"Let's see the garden first," says Ashley.

The willow tree is drooping.
The flowers are bending.

Ashley taps the hollyhocks.
The flowers pop up, scattering raindrops
like tiny glass beads onto the grass.

Rebecca taps the roses.
Raindrops and rose petals shower down on her feet.

Laughing, the girls duck under the willow.
Ashley stops.

"What are you doing?" asks Rebecca.
"Shh, do you hear?"
"I don't hear anything."
"I know. The rain isn't pattering on
our umbrella anymore."

The girls look up.
The willow tree spreads around them like
a giant green umbrella.

Ashley watches the raindrops slide down
the willow branches.
The raindrops drip and drop, drip and drop,
making puddles in the grass around the tree.
But they don't drip on Ashley.

"I've got an idea," she says.
She grabs the yellow umbrella and runs back
to the hollyhocks.
She picks two blossoms and two buds.

"What are you doing?" shouts Rebecca.
"It's raining."
"It's pouring!" says Ashley.
She fills the umbrella with water from
the rainspout
and runs back to the willow tree.

"Look, Rebecca!"
Carefully, Ashley sticks a hollyhock bud
onto the stem of each blossom.
"I've made dolls for us," she says.
"Hollyhock dolls."

Ashley puts the flower dolls in the water
and pushes them with her finger.
The dolls float inside the yellow umbrella.

Rain, rain stay all day.
Ashley doesn't care.
She and Rebecca are playing hollyhock dolls
under the willow umbrella.